Mermaids
Save the Oceans

Written by Terrilyn Kerr
Illustrated by Nancy Perkins

ISBN 978-1-987852-33-2

Published by Wood Islands Prints/Tom Schultz; 670 TCH, Route 1; Wood Islands, PE, C0A 1R0; Canada; schultz@pei.sympatico.ca

Terrilyn has continued to write about the Atlantic ocean and life in and around it, enjoying the beauty of each season. She grew up on the Prairies and moved to the East Coast fifty-five years ago, eventually making her home in Prince Edward Island. She has explored traditional and modern crafts and has expanded her hobbies. Writing, rug braiding, beading and rug hooking are some of her favourites. Terrilyn lives with her husband beside their daughter where they can see the ocean and be inspired by its changing beauty.
Terrilynkerr@gmail.com, Terrilynkerr.ca (website)

Nancy Perkins is a painter of nautical themes. She works in oils and acrylics. The illustrations in the book are in mixed media. Her work is in Island galleries, private collections and is included in the PEI Provincial Art Bank. She is retired from gallery display but continues to paint. She lives in Montague in the winter and Little Sands in the summer.
nancyperkinspainter@hotmail.com

In memory of
Diane Lynn Blumberg,
the most beautiful mermaid

I am grateful for my husband, Sandy,
his editing skills and continuing support.
I am thankful for my family and friends
and for their loving encouragement.
For my two beautiful mermaids,
Sophie and Gabby,
I will always be eternally grateful.

Diane the Wise was the queen of the mermaids. She was very beautiful, and the mermaids from all over the world looked to her for guidance. She had long, flowing red hair but recently, as she swam through the oceans, garbage had been getting tangled in her hair. Not only that, Queen Diane had begun to feel ill because of the toxins in the water. The mermaid Queen was annoyed and very frustrated! This garbage had been piling up on the ocean floor for years but now it seemed to be reaching a stage where it was affecting the health of all of the ocean dwellers.

Some humans had been trying to stop the discarding of this ocean garbage. However, most humans had little knowledge of, or cared about what lived under the ocean and seas of the world. It also seemed that the world governments were more helpful to the large corporations and their profit-making schemes than the health and welfare of the world. Something had to be done! Since the oceans were the home of many different affected species, the Queen realized that it was now up to the ocean dwellers to come together to solve this problem. Humans needed to be taught that their habit of dumping what they didn`t want into the waters was harming not only ocean lives, but their own lives as well.

Queen Diane decided to send her messenger dolphins to gather reports from all the mermaid nations, about the size and scope of the problem. Within a week, she had received the troubling replies. Human-made garbage was everywhere and covered 88% of the seas. Cars, tires, food wrappers, beverage bottles, grocery bags, straws and take out containers, all made of plastics and metals were piling up in the oceans.

Abandoned fishing nets, called ghost nets, were found to be amongst the worst large pollutants.

One little girl was overheard telling her friend not to worry about any trash thrown into the waters, because her daddy told her the oceans would take it away! However, every day small fish and large mammals were dying as they accidentally ate plastics, ingested toxins, or became entangled in human fishing gear.

Humans couldn`t seem to understand the wonders that the oceans contained such as mountains, valleys and vegetation, and they couldn`t see how necessary the oceans were for life itself. They didn`t know that the oceans produce over 70 percent of the earth`s surface and regulate climate and weather patterns.

Once the reports had come in, the Queen decided that action needed to be taken immediately! A large assembly of mermaids, dolphins, whales, sharks and other large and small fish, sea horses, lobsters, turtles and crabs was called. They came from all over the world to tell their stories and offer solutions. All of the animals had a turn speaking, and Queen Diane found that the situation was far more dreadful than anyone had realized.

The whales told of their families being tangled in fishing gear left floating as garbage.

The fish told of becoming sick from eating colourful plastics, thinking it was food.

The dolphins and sea turtles told of swimming through some areas of the seas and becoming stuck, unable to move because of all the floating garbage.

The sharks told of the toxins spewed out from human factories and of pollution flowing into the seas.

Everyone had a horror story to tell!

As they listened to everyone`s stories, the mermaids and the other animals became very angry. They knew that some humans were trying their best to stop all the pollution, but not enough were involved in the solution. If only humans could see all the trash under the seas that the ocean inhabitants could see!

Then two mermaids, Sophie and Gabrielle, came up with an idea! Why not move some of the nets, plastics and garbage back on to specific land sites around the world? Then the humans could see just how much their garbage was filling up the oceans. The other creatures of the seas and oceans loved their idea and cheered.

Queen Diane welcomed their idea and began to organize the great assembly. The specific ocean regions were divided into sections and everyone cooperated with each other to begin this wonderful plan.

The mermaids from the waters around the Far East and Australia organized their section. With help from the local sea creatures they formalized their plan to recover the garbage.

Both groups of mermaids from the icy Southern and Cold North Atlantic joined together and asked the Antarctic and Arctic animals to help scoop up their trash and throw it onto the land.

The rest of the moderate Atlantic and Pacific Oceans` mermaids and animals decided to work together over that vast area and toss garbage onto the shore.

When Queen Diane gave the signal, everyone around the world's oceans and seas began to scoop up the trash, plastics, nets, paper, wood, metal and nets. The blue whales were able to take enormous amounts into their mouths, swim to shore, and spit them onto the land. The smaller fish, seals and dolphins dragged nets, plastic cartons and bottles to shore and left them there. The giant squids carried multiple containers in their arms, and threw their trash onto the land. The inhabitants of the seas and oceans worked day and night to return to the land what the humans had thrown into the water.

As the trash began to pile up on the land, groups of humans from all over the world began to realize what was happening - and they were horrified! They had no idea that the amount of trash they had thrown into the ocean was so huge! They also did not want all that trash on their land!

They began to change their ways, make new laws, and stop pollution. They started to use their garbage wisely by creating items such as fence posts, benches, kitchenware, and trash bags out of all their recycled plastics.They even began to make houses out of recycled plastics! Humans stopped throwing the cups, drinking straws, plates, bags and ropes into the ocean and onto the land. Governments enforced the new laws with large fines if corporations dumped toxins into the waterways.

Meanwhile, the oceans and seas gradually became cleaner, and the mermaids and other ocean folk were so happy that the humans had listened to them and changed their ways. Queen Diane decided that the whole world deserved a big celebration for all their efforts, and she invited the humans to celebrate with the ocean inhabitants.

All over the world and under the waters everyone got together and partied.

The Krakens held up their arms for mermaids and humans to dive off. Whales gave rides to everyone, penguins danced on the land, the albatross and flying fish swooped and dropped colourful leaves and seaweed onto the partiers.

SIGHTSEEING TOURS TODAY

PEANUT BUTTER + JELLYFISH WRAP

FRIED EGG JELLY FISH MUFFIN

SEAWEED PIE

At last the whole world began to show a cleaner environment. Not only did the humans look after the oceans, they also took care of the land. They planted trees, stopped cutting the rainforests, planted more gardens and cleaned up the toxins from industries.The air became easier to breathe and people learned to treasure not only their own land but also the oceans.

The Mermaids and ocean folk became friends with the humans and land animals. They worked with each other every day to care for the earth and oceans.

Once a year there was a worldwide celebration, and everyone renewed their pledges to look after our beautiful world.

WIKIPEDIA INFORMATION

MERMAID: is a mythical, aquatic creature with the head and upper body of a female human and the tail of a fish. Mermaids appear in the folklore of many cultures worldwide, including Europe, Asia, and Africa.

OCEANS: The oceans cover more than 70 percent of the surface of our planet. It's hard to imagine, but about 97 percent of the Earth's water can be found in our oceans. Of the tiny percentage that's not in the oceans, about two percent is frozen up in glaciers and ice caps.

GHOSTGEAR: Abandoned fishing gear, called "ghost gear", continues to catch creatures as if they were still being used, snaring and entangling species that cannot free themselves and end up dying. This damages both marine life and the fisherman who lose part of their potential catch.

OXYGEN: At least half of Earth's oxygen comes from the oceans. Scientists estimate that 50-80% of the oxygen production on Earth comes from the oceans. The majority of this production is from oceanic plankton—drifting plants, algae, and some bacteria that can photosynthesize.

PLASTICS IN THE OCEAN: Plastic is everywhere: In your home, your office, your school—and your ocean. Among the top 10 kinds of trash picked up during the <u>2017 International Coastal Cleanup</u> were food wrappers, beverage bottles, grocery bags, straws, and take out containers, all made of plastic.

OTHER POLLUTION: Chemical pollution is the introduction of harmful contaminants. Common man-made pollutants that reach the ocean include pesticides, herbicides, fertilizers, detergents, oil, industrial chemicals, and sewage. Many ocean pollutants are released into the environment far upstream from coastlines.

Ten Simple Things You Can Do to Help Protect the Earth

- Reduce, Reuse, and Recycle. Cut down on what you throw away. Follow the three "R's" to conserve natural resources and landfill space.

- Volunteer. Volunteer for cleanups in your community. You can get involved in protecting your watershed, too.

- Educate—when you further your own education, you can help others understand the importance and value of our natural resources.

- Conserve water. The less water you use, the less runoff and waste water eventually end up in the ocean.

- Choose sustainable—learn how to make smart seafood choices at www.fishwatch.gov.

- Shop wisely. Buy less plastic and bring a reusable shopping bag.

- Use long-lasting light bulbs—energy efficient light bulbs reduce greenhouse gas emissions. Also, flip the light switch off when you leave the room!

- Plant a tree. Trees provide food and oxygen. They help save energy, clean the air, and help combat climate change.

- Don't send chemicals into our waterways. Choose non-toxic chemicals in the home and office.

- Bike more. Drive less.